STRIVE TO SURVIVE
YOU DECIDE WHAT HAPPENS

Escape!

Written by
Jeanne Gowen Dennis and Sheila Seifert

Cover illustration by David Hohn
Interior illustrations by Ron Adair

www.cookcommunications.com/kidz

Faith
Building
Guide
Ages
9 and up
Courage

Faith Kidz® is an imprint of Cook Communications Ministries
Colorado Springs, Colorado 80918
Cook Communications, Paris, Ontario
Kingsway Communications, Eastbourne, England

ESCAPE!
©2003 by Jeanne Gowen Dennis and Sheila Seifert

First printing, 2003
Printed in U.S.A.
1 2 3 4 5 6 7 8 9 10 Printing/Year 07 06 05 04 03

Senior Editor: Heather Gemmen
Design Manager: Jeffrey P. Barnes
Designer: Granite Design

Have you ever wanted to witness the Red Sea opening or the walls of Jericho falling? The Strive to Survive series takes you into the middle of the action of your favorite Bible stories.

In each story, you are the main character. What happens is up to you! Through your choices, you can receive great rewards, get into big trouble, or even lose your life.

Your goal is to choose well and survive.
Your adventure begins now.

Escape!

"Come on!" Beker shouts. Beker is the best thief in all of Jerusalem. No one has ever caught her long, slender fingers taking a single coin.

"This crowd is enormous," Mahol says. "We're going to eat well tonight." Mahol is the brains of your group. He is tall and can talk his way out of almost anything. He continues, "Now's our chance to lighten a few purses."

You have survived because you run fast.

Ever since you can remember you have been an orphan. You and dozens of other orphans live on the streets of Jerusalem. You steal together and do whatever is necessary to survive.

Mahol, Beker, and you work your way down the street. When you get near the crowd, you split up and blend in. The sweat of so many people all in one place fills the air around you. The people are shouting, "Hosanna! Blessed is he who comes in the name of the Lord."

They are shouting to a man riding a donkey.

Some people are calling him a king, but he looks poor to you. You are about to steal a stout man's coins from a soft pouch when you hear someone say, "Jesus healed me from being blind. Hosanna!" You look. The man next to you is blind Matthias, but now he can see. How can that be?

You have heard of this Jesus. You heard that he did many miracles—healed diseases and fed thousands of people with only a little food. Some say he even brought a dead man back to life. Perhaps they will crown him king.

You push through the crowd to see him better. He looks straight at you. His eyes are gentle, and it feels as if he knows you. You shake your head. You have never seen him before in your life.

"He is the Messiah! Hosanna!" shouts a woman. You look at the ground. You don't want to steal from this crowd. Later that night, Mahol shares a piece of bread with you so you do not go hungry.

A few days later Beker tells you, "Do you remember that Jesus fellow we saw on the donkey?" You nod, and she continues, "He was arrested."

"By Rome?" you ask.

She shakes her head. "No, the Council."

The next day, the streets are clogged with people. You hear women weeping. The crowd parts for Roman soldiers. You can tell by the nails one soldier is carrying that there is to be a crucifixion, but why are they using nails today? Sometimes they use only ropes. The criminal being crucified must have done something terribly wrong. You shudder at the thought of people dying so cruelly. It has always been one of your biggest fears that you might be caught and then crucified. Crucifixion is too horrible to watch.

You start to leave, but then you hear someone cry out, "Jesus!" You look at the man who has just fallen under a cross. His face is torn and bleeding. How can anyone tell who he is? He looks at you, and you recognize the kindness in his eyes. You let the crowd push you toward Golgotha, where Jesus is nailed to the cross beside two other crucified men. Somehow you just cannot bring yourself to steal from anyone today.

After a few days, you are stealing for your daily bread again. One day, after an especially big heist, Beker says, "Did you hear the latest? People are saying that Jesus rose from the dead."

"Yeah, right," you say.

Beker laughs.

It has been weeks since you heard the resurrection rumors. Today a lot of foreigners are in Jerusalem. You walk toward a noisy crowd listening to some men talk.

Your friend Mahol says, "Big crowds mean big pickings."

"I wonder what's going on," you say.

"Who cares?" Mahol answers and moves into the midst of the crowd, on the lookout for easy coins.

When he is gone, a woman turns to you. "Those men are Jesus' disciples. Everyone listening is hearing them in their own language."

You give her a strange look.

"I know it doesn't make sense," she says, "but it's true. The one speaking over there is named Peter." You edge closer to listen. Peter talks about Jesus. What Peter says makes sense to you—the kindness in Jesus' eyes, his death, and his resurrection.

CHOICE ONE: If you find yourself believing in Jesus as God, go to page 9.

CHOICE TWO: If you go back to stealing, go to page 11.

No lightning struck, but you suddenly know that you are changed in some huge way.

The woman who spoke to you earlier puts a hand on your shoulder. "Why don't you come over for dinner."

You eat dinner with Anna, her husband, Joshua, and their two girls. You end up staying with them for several weeks, becoming a welcome part of their family. You begin to understand Jesus' love even more through them. Now you are one of Jesus' followers, too.

Today you are helping Stephen, another follower of Jesus, get food ready for some widows. You watch him work. Stephen is not afraid of anyone. He speaks boldly about Jesus and has done many miracles in Jesus' name. You hope to be like Stephen someday.

"Make sure Hannah gets her bread," he says. He hands you two loaves of warm bread. You nod and tie them into your cloak.

Suddenly four guards walk to where Stephen is and grab him. "What are you doing?" You are knocked to the side.

"Is the kid with him?" one of the guards asks. His voice is rough and without emotion.

As two guards drag Stephen away, the other two turn toward you. You dart through the crowd to escape. They follow you.

CHOICE ONE: If you lose the guards and then go to Hannah's, go to page **12.**

CHOICE TWO: If you lose the guards and then decide never to go near those dangerous followers of Jesus again, go to page **16.**

CHOICE THREE: If you lose the guards and then go for help, go to page **18.**

You ignore what Peter says and steal enough money for a great dinner. After a few more weeks of taking small money pouches, you break into a rich man's house. A bag of coins is lying beside the man's bed. You sneak into the room. The man's snores are steady. You creep up to where his hand rests beside his moneybag. As you reach for the bag, the man snorts and turns toward you. You dive behind a chair. Whew! He is still asleep. You return to his side, lift the bag, and quietly creep out of the room.

Setting your bag on the floor, you hike your leg over the windowsill. When you reach back for the bag, you find that it is heavier. You can't budge it. Suddenly a tingling feeling runs down your spine. The rich man is standing beside you. His foot is holding the bag.

You have visions of being crucified, but the man takes you into his house. His name is Joseph of Arimathea. He becomes your family and teaches you about Jesus. He takes you to see the empty tomb, the same tomb that he let Jesus use for his burial. Finally, you become a believer. You never steal again.

THE END

You dodge past people and into the maze of Jerusalem's streets, just like you used to do with Mahol and Beker. Left at the tax collector's stand. Right behind the potter's shed. Left through the alley behind Rabbi Levi's home. Two rights, and you scrape your back on a rock that juts out. You crawl through a hole into a deserted courtyard. You wait.

Footsteps hurry past your hiding place. You wait. They come back, slower this time. Not until they have walked past you a third time do you ease yourself out of the hole.

Quickly you make your way to Hannah's house. You knock on her door and untie the bread. Its fragrance leaps back into the air as if nothing had happened. She recognizes you from the gatherings of believers and lets you in.

"These are from Stephen," you tell her. "He's been arrested."

She nods sadly. "I'll pray for him."

"They were after me, too, but I got away. I'm going to go find out what has happened to Stephen."

"I'll pray for you, too," she says.

You race across the city and to the Temple. Just outside the doorway to the Sanhedrin, you see a young Temple guard who is a believer.

"What's happening in there?" you ask.

"They accused Stephen of speaking against the Temple and the Law."

"How can they say that?" you demand.

"They're all lies. But he stayed so calm. I saw

his face glow like an angel. He's in there now talking about everything from Abraham to Jesus of Nazareth." You both stop to listen, but the voices sound muffled to you, and you can only understand an occasional word.

You hear an uproar from the Council Room. "What did Stephen say? What's going on? I couldn't hear."

Your friend stifles a smile. "He called the Council stiff-necked, uncircumcised, and murderers."

You shake your head. "They're not going to like that." You lean a hand against the smooth wall beside you. Suddenly the whole Council erupts with shouting. It sounds like dozens of two-year-olds throwing tantrums.

You edge closer and hear Stephen's voice over the crowd. "Look, I see heaven open and the Son of Man standing at the right hand of God." You and the guard look up, but you only see the sky.

Men suddenly burst out of the chamber. Your friend pulls you to the side. The faces of the Council men are bulging into deep red and purple colors.

"Blasphemer!" they shout. "Stone him!"

Stephen must be somewhere in the middle of those angry voices. You hurry to keep up with them. They are heading outside the city. They really are going to stone Stephen! You follow and then stand helplessly by as men lay their robes down at the feet of the man standing next to you. He's obviously a leader.

People pick up stones and start throwing them at Stephen. Big ones. Small ones. When they hit Stephen's body, you cringe. Thunk! Thunk! Crack! You wonder if Stephen's bones are breaking, yet Stephen's face is glowing. You wish there were a way for you to help him escape, but the rocks keep coming.

Someone comes over to talk to the man beside you. "Well, Saul," he says. "It's good to be rid of one blasphemer."

Saul smiles. "We're just getting started." A chill runs down your back. You have a bitter taste in your mouth. The rocks are flying faster and faster at Stephen. He cannot possibly survive.

Wait! Stephen is saying something. "Lord Jesus, receive my spirit." He drops to his knees. "Lord, do not hold this sin against them." He slumps to the ground.

CHOICE ONE: If you scream, "No!" go to page 29.

CHOICE TWO: If you force yourself to keep quiet, go to page 69.

You hurry through the gates of Jerusalem and head for the hills nearby. You find a cave for shelter. Its coolness is refreshing. Sheep graze on a hillside not too far away. After days in your new location, and when your stomach is so empty it hurts, you find their owner.

"I'd like to watch your sheep for you in return for food," you say.

The owner looks you over. "I had a good shepherd, but he was a follower of Jesus of Nazareth. He left when he heard that a man was stoned to death for believing."

Stoned to death? Could he mean Stephen? The news shocks you, but you do not let the man know. It could be dangerous to tell him that you are also a follower of Jesus.

"How long would you stay?" the man asks.

"I'll stay as long as I can. Will you teach me how to care for your sheep?"

The man agrees. You live in a shepherd's hut and keep the sheep safe. You enjoy a bowl of lamb stew almost every day. When travelers pass by, which is not too often, you share what you have with them.

One day a man passes through the area who you recognize as a follower of Jesus from Jerusalem. You give Palti food and a place to stay. He does not seem to recognize you.

"How did you get those bruises?" you ask.

"Saul and his men have gone crazy. They beat

up the followers of Jesus and throw many of them into prison. They've even killed some. I'm headed elsewhere."

"I used to know a family who lived in Jerusalem," you say casually. "The man's name was Joshua, and his wife's name was Anna. They were followers of Jesus. Did you know them?"

Palti shakes his head. "If they haven't left the city, then they are probably in prison—or dead."

Your heart feels heavy.

CHOICE ONE: If you leave with Palti when he goes, go to page 92.

CHOICE TWO: If you return to Jerusalem to find Joshua's family, go to page 32.

You hurry home and tell Joshua, "Stephen is in trouble. They've arrested him. What should we do?"

"I don't know," Joshua says. "We'll try to find one of the apostles. You check the marketplace, and I'll head toward the Temple."

You agree and take off running. Peter and John are always preaching somewhere. They should be easy to find. You run throughout Jerusalem all morning. Today, you cannot find them anywhere. When you arrive home, Joshua has already returned.

"I couldn't find anyone," you say.

In a serious voice, Joshua says, "Sit down."

You sit on a stool. "What happened?"

"Stephen is dead," Joshua says.

Your mind feels jumbled and confused. "What? But I was with him just a little while ago. There has to be some mistake!"

"He was stoned to death," Anna says.

"Stoned to death? Why? He didn't do anything wrong." You run your fingers through your hair. This cannot be happening.

"Stephen was condemned for blasphemy against God, the Law of Moses, and the Temple," Joshua says.

"But Stephen never showed any disrespect for God or holy things."

"In the eyes of the Council, it is wrong to believe that Jesus is the Son of God."

"Then that makes everyone who believes in Jesus a criminal." A new kind of fear fills your heart.

"If they killed Stephen, then what will keep them from killing us, too?"

"Nothing," Anna says.

"We're thinking about moving," says Joshua.

You look at Rachel playing on the floor and Naomi cuddling her doll and agree. "It's our only option."

Joshua rubs his beard. "You know the guards at the gates and how they do things. Should we leave immediately or wait until tonight?"

CHOICE ONE: If you advise the family to leave tonight, go to page 59.

CHOICE TWO: If you urge the family to pack and leave immediately, go to page 78.

Although you feel awful for Simeon, your family is counting on you. They must come first. You climb to the rooftop and put the ropes in place. You scout out possible avenues of escape. When your family arrives, everything is ready. They are somber. Even little Rachel is silent. Your heart aches for how much they must give up as they leave Jerusalem.

"The children first," Joshua whispers. You nod. Together, you lower Naomi.

Before you lower Rachel, she leans forward and gives you a hug. "I love you." You kiss her soft cheek and then lower her to where Naomi is waiting. Without another word, you work to get Anna over the wall and safely down to her children.

You and Joshua use both ropes to lower the family's possessions—but then you hear a noise. Soldiers are marching nearby. You both duck into the hay where you have been standing. It smells moldy, as if it needs to be tossed out. You wait for the soldiers to pass. It seems to take ages. There is time to look up into the heavens at the stars blinking through the darkened night. You are amazed at God's handiwork.

Joshua nudges you. "They're gone. We'd better hurry before the tenants come up to stargaze or get rainwater to drink."

You give him a smile. "I know we should be terrified by all of this, but somehow when I know God is with us, nothing seems quite as bad."

Joshua pats your back. "You go next."

"No," you say. "I know how to climb down the wall without a rope. Besides, if I don't make it, you can still take care of the family. Think of them."

"God has done such a work in your heart," Joshua says.

Slowly you let Joshua down. Just as he reaches the ground, you hear the sound of footsteps. Someone is on the roof. Quickly you untie the rope so that it falls to the ground next to Joshua. You know he will understand. You dart under the hay again. A second coil of rope is lying on the roof not far from where you are hiding. You forgot to kick it under the hay. You hold your breath.

The newcomer is a man. He paces back and forth on his rooftop as if he is in deep thought. In his wanderings, he eventually trips over the rolled rope.

"Where did this come from?" he says aloud. He picks it up, examines it, and then carries it back toward the steps to the house. You hear him say, "Martha, where did we get this rope?" The door shuts behind him.

You must leave quickly before he returns. You rush back to the wall, and slowly slide over the top. You begin to climb down. One foot. One hand. One foot. One hand. You are only halfway down when it happens. Your foot slips and yanks your hand from its perch. You frantically grab for the wall, but your hand slices through the empty air. You feel yourself falling.

Your breath is knocked out of you when you land, but you do not feel any pain. You hear voices whispering around you. It takes a moment for you to realize that you did not hit the ground. You are in Joshua's arms. He caught you. You want to shout your thanks, but you know that you must be quiet. You give him a bear hug to show him how grateful you are.

You and your family escape without any other problems. You start a new life in another village. You tell everyone about Jesus and how he can change their lives, just as he did for you.

THE END

When Beker leaves, you find a merchant's cart, half-filled with hay, parked near you. You dive into the hay and hope that the merchant will be leaving Jerusalem soon. The hay is prickly against your skin, but you ignore it. You are extremely tired. You close your eyes.

When you wake up, the cart is moving. You peek out of the hay from the back of the wagon. It is night. You cannot tell where you are, but you know that you must be quite a distance from Jerusalem. It is dangerous to be alone at night, so you stay in the warm hay. The rocking motion of the cart lulls you back to sleep.

The next time you wake up, the cart has stopped. You cautiously slide yourself out of the wagon. It is parked in the back of a small farm. You shake the hay out of your hair, walk to the small house, and knock on the door. A woman with small eyes and a scowl on her mouth opens it.

You ask, "Do you have work I can do for food?" The smell of sweet bread greets you from the house.

The woman snorts. "Go away!"

"Who is it?" asks a friendly male voice.

"Another beggar."

"I'm looking for honest work," you call out to the man.

"A beggar?" He comes to the door. "You're just a child. Have you ever worked on a farm?"

You shake your head no, and say, "But I'm a

good learner."

"This urchin is of no value to us," says the woman. "Children eat too much anyway."

"Children are a blessing from the Lord," the man says. He turns to you. "Why don't you go and fetch some water from the well." He points across the yard. "And then we'll talk."

You smile and run to the well. You'll never have to steal again.

THE END

The next day, you and Mahol find a way to leave Jerusalem. Mahol shows you how to hide in a large earthenware jar and ride out of the city. Your legs cramp inside of the vessel as you bounce along. The inside of the jar is rough as you bump against it. The wagon keeps going for a very long time. When it stops, you find yourself in Bethlehem. By that time you can no longer feel your feet. You try to get out of the jar, but you have to move slowly. Your legs sting and tingle as the blood flows back into them. It takes a while before your legs feel normal.

Mahol glances around. "This looks just like Jerusalem." You eye him strangely. Bethlehem looks nothing like Jerusalem. Bethlehem's market is not as large, and the odor of animal droppings is barely noticeable. He sighs and sits down. "I guess this isn't the type of change that I was looking for."

Do you dare mention what you are thinking? Silently, you pray, "God, I need your help."

Out loud, you say, "Maybe the change that you're looking for is on the inside."

He rolls his eyes. "You'd have to cut me open for a change like that."

"That's not what I meant. I'm a follower of Jesus, and he changed my heart."

Mahol does not look surprised. "I knew there was something different about you."

You tell him everything you learned from the apostles, Joshua, and Stephen. He asks all kinds of questions. Finally, Mahol accepts Jesus as his

Messiah, too.

You enjoy your time in Bethlehem together. During the day, you glean for grain on the edges of fields. You can chew on a handful of grain for quite a while. It seems like you always have food in your mouth. In the evening, you talk about God.

One day, Mahol grabs your arm. "We can't just stay here. We have to tell others about Jesus."

"Where do you want to go?" you ask.

"Back to Jerusalem. I want to tell all the other street kids about Jesus," he says.

CHOICE ONE: If you go with Mahol, go to page 76.

CHOICE TWO: If you leave to find your family, go to page 65.

You lower your voice. "I am a follower of Jesus. They just killed a believer named Stephen. I can't go home, because I don't want anyone to follow me there. I'm willing to die for my beliefs, and I know everyone in my family is, too. But if I can keep them alive by not going home, I will."

"I see," Mahol says. "I don't know about all this religious stuff, but I'll tell your family to get out."

"Thank you," you say.

When Mahol leaves, you follow him at a distance. You weave through the market stands filled with bread, duck, and fish so that he does not know you are following him. You pray that you did not make a mistake by telling him the truth. You do not want him to report your family to the Council.

He heads toward your house. When he gets close to where your family lives, you are satisfied. You lean against the rough walls of a house and take a deep breath before you turn toward the gates of Jerusalem. As you leave, no one seems to notice you.

You wait in the hills nearby for a few days, but you do not see your family leave Jerusalem. Finally, you take the road to Samaria and find work doing odd jobs for people. You are surprised at how nice people are when you are helpful. You begin to make new friends. They do not mind your talking about Jesus. Some of them even ask you questions about him.

A few months later, you are drawing water for a widow. You hear a familiar voice. "I'm thirsty." It is

Rachel. You run over, pick her up, and swing her around in a circle.

"I've found you!" you say. Still holding Rachel, you embrace Joshua, Anna, and Naomi.

"What about me?" It is Mahol's voice.

"Mahol?" You set Rachel down and give Mahol an enormous hug.

"What are you doing here?" you ask. Mahol looks unsure of himself. This surprises you.

Joshua laughs. "He came and told us what you said. Then he asked to know more about Jesus."

Mahol shrugs. "Since you thought he was worth dying for, I thought I ought to find out more about him."

You give him another hug. "I am so glad. First you were my brother in the streets. Now you are my brother in Christ."

THE END

You scream, "No!" You cannot believe that these angry men have killed your friend. You try to go to him, but the crowd is too thick and keeps you from moving forward.

A little voice in the back of your head asks, "What if they stone you, too?" You have to get away.

You struggle free from the crowd. With tears in your eyes, you run back to the city, down the narrow streets to where your family lives. By the time you get there, you are sobbing. The taste of salt from your tears is on your tongue.

"They've killed him! They've killed Stephen!"

Your family gathers around you—Rachel, Naomi, Joshua, and Anna. Anna puts her arms around you. She smells like the lentil soup that she has been making.

"Angry men drove Stephen from the city and stoned him to death," you tell them. A worried look passes between Anna and Joshua.

Joshua says, "It's only the beginning."

That night, you hear guards outside of your family's door. You peek through the window and notice Saul leading them. Did he follow you here?

CHOICE ONE: If you escape through a window, go to page 44.

CHOICE TWO: If you fling the door open and fight, go to page 62.

You shout and pretend to stumble backward, toppling over the stand with birds and lambs. The squawking and commotion turn the guards' attention toward you. You grasp a handful of feathers to catch a fowl. Looking at the guards, you act like you are going to steal it, then you drop it. Quickly you run away from the market, hoping that you have given Joshua enough time to get through the gate.

You know the guards are chasing after you. Their footsteps pound in your ears as you dodge through streets and into alleys. You even go over two rooftops, but you cannot seem to lose them. Then you take a wrong turn, and you find yourself in a dead end. It will be only moments until the guards reach you. As you catch your breath, the animal odor on your clothes make you gag.

Then you see Mahol and Beker.

CHOICE ONE: If you call to them for help, go to page 58.

CHOICE TWO: If you get out of the alley so that the guards do not grab your friends, go to page 79.

You go to the owner of the sheep and tell him the truth. "I am a follower of Jesus. When we first met, I was running away from Jerusalem and those who wanted to kill me because of my new faith in God." You smell the lamb stew and know that you may never get another bowl of it.

Your boss nods. "I was praying for you. I did not know the source of your struggles, but I knew that you had many to face. Tell me about this Jesus that you follow."

You tell him about Jesus' life, death, and resurrection.

"I always thought the Messiah would come as a mighty ruler," he says, "but the power Jesus showed was greater than any king's."

"So you believe that Jesus was raised from the dead and can forgive your sins?"

"Yes, I do. I know he is the Messiah, and I want to follow him. Now if you'll excuse me, I want to pray about this."

"Welcome to God's family," you say with a smile. You go back to watching the sheep for the rest of the afternoon.

With your boss's blessings, you leave for Jerusalem the next day. Your stomach feels jittery, but God's peace settles on your heart as you enter the city gates. When you arrive at your family's house, you knock. Strangers answer the door.

"Do you know where Joshua and Anna went?" you ask.

"They were killed along with their children,"

the owners say. As you walk away from the house, sadness fills your heart. You wish you could have been with them at the end.

You can hear the squawking of birds from the market when a voice says, "Is that the one?"

"It is!" says a man who used to be your neighbor.

Guards roughly grab you. You do not try to resist. They bring you before the Council. Strangers come before the Council and say, "I heard this child speak against God and his holy Temple!"

"Listen," you say. "All I know is that Jesus saved me from my sin. He wants to save you, too. He's not dead anymore. He is the Messiah that we've all been waiting for. He's the Son of the Living God."

"Blasphemer!" they shout. Your words have caused an uproar, but you barely hear the angry voices around you. Hands drag you out of the building, down the street, and out of Jerusalem. Peace, stronger than anything you have ever felt, washes over you. You pray for the people around you. If only they would come to know Jesus, too.

When people begin throwing stones at you, they hurt, but not as much as you expected. You look up and see the kingdom of heaven opening before you. You are astounded at the beauty! And Jesus is there. This time he shines brighter than lightning. You would be frightened, but you see him smiling at you. Kindness glows from his eyes.

You leave your body and fly straight into Jesus' arms.

THE END

You whisper, "Go quickly."

Shomer nods and moves away with Maacah. You glance behind you. Maacah's hysterics are growing.

"Oh no! Soldiers! Run, Simeon!" you call as if Simeon is in the alley in front of you. You dart into the alley.

You can hear the soldiers' yelling, "They went that way." As you round a corner, you smell horse droppings. You saw a man loading the dung into a cart earlier. The soldiers are gaining. You can hear the pounding of their feet.

You knock over a water jar and push a pile of the dung into the street where the soldiers will pass. Turning quickly, you climb the side of a building. You reach the top just as the soldiers reach the manure. They slip on it and fall down. When they regain their footing, they continue the chase, unaware that you are no longer in front of them.

You race across rooftops back to Simeon's house. You guide him to the escape wall. A rope is hanging over it. You smile. Your family must have gotten away safely! You and Simeon climb down. When your feet touch the ground, you laugh quietly. You have escaped! Although neither you nor Simeon is touching the rope, it moves. Someone is pulling on it!

"Thieves!" a man yells. "Help! Jerusalem is being attacked!" You and Simeon sprint away from the wall.

You trip on a ditch and hear, "Over there! Don't let them get away."

Simeon drops down beside you and motions for you to stay low. A cloud is about to cover the moon. When it does, you both run for another dip in the terrain. When the moon comes out, you see soldiers searching for you near the wall. You flatten yourselves against the hard dirt.

You point out a hill to Simeon. When another cloud covers the moon, you both run for it. From there, the soldiers do not find you.

Cautiously, you go to Bethlehem with Simeon.

Shomer tells you, "Your family is safe in Nazareth." You stay with Simeon until you hear a rumor that Saul has become a follower of Jesus. That disturbs you.

When you leave to find your family, you go to where Saul is first. Saul's name is now Paul, and he is preaching about Jesus. You struggle with your feelings. This man killed Stephen. Then you remember your own sins.

You walk up to Paul. "Somehow Jesus forgave me. I'm going to have to forgive you."

"Thank you," Paul says. "God is amazing." His eyes are shining with such a love that you know without any doubt that Paul is your brother in Christ Jesus.

THE END

You do not answer him. You go to your family's home and help them pack. They take whatever they can carry.

"Where is your pack?" Joshua asks.

"I'm not going with you," you say.

"There's no future here," Joshua says.

You shrug. "Maybe not, but there are a lot of people who might need help."

Joshua nods. "That is very brave of you." You see him wavering, as if he would like to stay and help.

"You, on the other hand, have a family," you say.

Joshua smiles. "And I must take them to safety." You both hug. Anna looks as if she will cry as she kisses you goodbye. You can smell a large pot of lentil soup that she has left behind for you.

When they leave, you are alone. You waste no time. You have been studying the prison for days. You follow Saul around town. The angry lines in his face tell you that he needs the peace that you have found in the Lord. He does not see you as you slide in and out of alleys. Mahol and Beker see you though. It feels good to be around your friends again. It is as if you never left.

One day you hear that Hannah's house will be raided next. You find Mahol.

"Please, will you help me warn a friend that Saul's men are on their way to her house? She's a widow near the old wall. Her name's Hannah," you say.

Mahol nods. "Sure. I like Hannah."

"You know Hannah?" You are surprised.

Mahol smiles. "She caught me stealing bread from her one day and has left out a slice for me every day since."

You smile. That sounds like Hannah. When Mahol leaves, you get to work. Saul and his men are headed for Hannah's house. You chase a flock of fowl into the street in front of them. The birds make a terrible racket with their squawking. Saul's men have to work their way around the birds. When they leave the fowl behind, you begin throwing pebbles at them from rooftops along their path. They stop to try to catch you, but you disappear into back alleys. You hear later that Hannah is safe.

Every day, you follow Saul's men and try to keep them from completing their job. One day as you are throwing pottery from the rooftops, a guard grabs you. He has been waiting for you there all day. He throws you into prison.

You do not care. You sing praises to God all day and night. You are surprised that your voice remains strong and loud. You have no desire to stop singing. They finally let you go, because you have a terrible singing voice.

THE END

You shrug. "Maybe they don't like my face."
They laugh. You continue, "I fell into a flock of birds
and got them all riled up."

The three of you hang out together, hiding in
Joshua's home and eating leftover food for a few
days. It begins tasting hard and stale, but you prefer
any kind of food to going hungry. You enter and
leave by a back window. You cannot help wonder-
ing what happened to your family. You want to
search for them.

One day, you say, "I'm leaving Jerusalem. I
want to start fresh somewhere else." You want to
search for your family.

Beker looks upset. "You'll never find the pickings as good as they are here."

"Maybe," you say, "but I won't know until I've
tried."

Mahol fingers a stale barley loaf. "I've been
thinking of making some changes, also."

Beker rolls her eyes. "Now I've heard everything."

"I'm serious," Mahol says. He looks at you. "I
feel restless. It's time for a change. Maybe I'll go with
you."

"Sounds good." You smile, but you do not feel
like smiling. If Mahol goes with you, he will eventually figure out that you are a believer in Jesus. This
could be dangerous for your family and you. It might
even be dangerous for him.

CHOICE ONE: If you leave with Mahol the next day, go to page 25.

CHOICE TWO: If you sneak away in the night and leave Mahol behind, go to page 84.

You shrug. You cannot endanger your family by telling Mahol the truth.

"I've got my reasons," you say. "Can I count on you?"

"I've got nothing better to do," Mahol says.

"You're the best, Mahol," you say.

He shrugs. "By the way, you look awful, something like the shepherds I just saw in the marketplace. Of course, you don't smell as bad as they do. Are you okay?"

You nod.

"I'll make sure your family's safe," Mahol says. "Trust me." You cannot help feeling a little worried.

You punch him in the arm. "Okay, if you say so."

He takes off in one direction, and you go in another. What he said gave you an idea. You head for the market and find the shepherds. They look just as messy as you do. You watch them shopping for food and can tell they need help. The person they are about to buy from always doubles the prices for people from out of town.

You go up to the one who looks like the leader and quietly say, "Don't buy from that stand."

He looks at you and raises his eyebrows. You know he wonders if you are a thief trying to trick him to get his money. Who knows? Maybe you did steal from him before you became a follower of Jesus.

You smile. "I'm not a thief. You are not from

here. I am, and I can show you where to buy better fruit at half the price."

"And what's in this for you?" he asks.

"I want to leave Jerusalem. If you will let me travel with you, I will feel safer."

He nods. "Not many people want to travel with shepherds. Where's the fruit?"

You lead them to the stands that have the best produce. When they leave Jerusalem, you go with them. No one ever notices shepherds, so the guards do not notice you. Your group joins other shepherds who stayed in the fields with the sheep. The flock is enormous.

You volunteer to help watch the sheep, and they give you a shift. After a few days, the leader says, "We are short-handed. Would you like to stay with us?"

"I would," you say. It is nice to be around good people and to have friends. You send up a prayer for your family's safety.

That night around the fire, an older shepherd in the group tells a story. "On a night like this when I was young, a wonderful thing happened."

"And we haven't heard this story before," one man says, laughing.

"Shh!" says another. "The new kid hasn't heard it. Besides, I want to hear it again."

The old man continues, "I was watching sheep with some others near Bethlehem. Suddenly there was light all around us and an angel appeared. I tell you, I was scared, so scared I thought my heart would stop beating. Trembling with fear, I was—"

"We know. You were afraid," the first man said. "Get on with the story."

"He, the angel, said, 'Don't be afraid.' Sure, that was easy for him to say. Then—I remember it like it was yesterday—he said, 'I bring you good news of great joy that will be for all the people. Today in the town of David a Savior has been born to you; he is Christ, the Lord.'"

The shepherd moves closer and looks straight at you.

"He was talking about the Messiah! Well, I tell you, I was shocked. Why would an angel come to us? And with such news! Can you believe it? He told us we'd find the baby not in a house or an inn, but in a feeding trough, a manger. I wondered why a mother would put her newborn in a place where cows and donkeys slobber. What if a cow got hungry in the night?"

"Go on, will you?" said the same shepherd. He stirred the fire and red hot ash rose in the air.

"Well, all at once, the whole sky was filled with angels, singing and praising God like nothing I'd ever heard before. Then just as fast, the sky was dark again. We all hurried to Bethlehem and found the stable. The baby was right where the angel said he'd be, all wrapped up in cloth. I think they cleaned the feed box out."

The youngest shepherd moved closer to the

storyteller. His face shone in the light of the fire. "Tell us the best part."

"It was when that baby looked at me that I knew. He was our Savior, come straight to us from God. Well, we couldn't help ourselves. The whole way back to the fields, we praised the Lord for what we had seen. I left for another town soon after that. When I returned a few years later, I heard that King Herod had killed all the boys in Bethlehem ages two and under. I've always wondered ...." His voice trails off.

Everyone is silent. You take a deep breath. "I know what happened to the baby. He grew up to be Jesus of Nazareth."

"The one the Romans killed?" one of the men asked.

You nod. "But he rose from the dead the third day afterward." You tell them everything you know about Jesus. "His death paid for all our sins. He made peace with God for us."

The old man's eyes lit up. A slow smile crossed his face. He nodded. "I believe." Then he stood up and threw out his arms. "Glory to God in the highest!"

THE END

Without a word to your family, you run to the window at the back of the house. You are afraid that you have put them all in danger. Maybe if the guards do not find you, they will leave your family alone. If they do arrest your family, you can help them escape, but only if you are free. You slide silently over the rough ledge of the window and blend into the darkness.

You whisper a quick prayer. "Help my family, please." You thank God that you got so much training about living on the streets. You climb to a nearby rooftop. You can see your family being taken away, even little Rachel. You follow them to see where they are taken. An urge deep inside of you wants to flee now, this very moment.

"I'm going to rescue my family first," you whisper to yourself. You are not sure where to turn, so you go to Hannah's house.

"I thought you might be back," she says. You are amazed that she does not reprimand you for the lateness of the hour or your messy appearance. She opens the door and then bars it behind you. She continues, "Are you hungry?"

You nod. She gives you part of the loaf that you brought to her earlier that day.

"You can sleep on that mat by the table," she says. "This can be your home until you have your family back."

How did she know? Your eyes are moist, and you feel yourself trembling. Hannah's arms feel warm and strong as she hugs you.

"Don't tell me where you go or what you do. Then they can't force or trick the information out of me."

You do not get much sleep. You roll onto your side, then your back, and then back to your side. All night you try to work out a plan to save your family.

CHOICE ONE: If you steal the keys to the prison door, go to page 80.

CHOICE TWO: If you spend your time praying, go to page 72.

You give Eleazar another smile, as you both enter the gates of Jerusalem. "Yes, I'll join you." You wonder if he sees through your pretense. Does he suspect that you intend to warn families of the raids so they will be able to escape?

Eleazar nods. "Meet me here just after dark tonight."

"Who will we catch first?" you ask. You stumble over a rut in the street.

"Just be here," he says. His lips turn up. You nod, but his thin, sinister smile makes you nervous. You take a roundabout way home, making certain that no one is following you.

When you arrive home, you pull Joshua aside. "They've killed Stephen, and now they're going to raid the homes of all the believers. We'll all go to prison, or worse. I'm going to pretend to be one of them. That way I can try to warn our friends in time."

Joshua shakes his head, "Your intentions are worthy, but what you're doing is a lie. It will come to no good."

You shrug. "Perhaps you should leave Jerusalem. It would be safer."

"Where would we go?" he asks. "No, this is our home. My family has lived here for generations." Even the smell of the ground that formed these walls has a sense of home to it. You nod.

Yet, fear for these dear people that you have come to love grips your heart. You must help save

them, somehow. That night, you meet Eleazar at the gate just after dark.

"Where are we headed?" you ask. Your teeth are chattering, but the weather is not even chilly.

"First, we meet Saul," he says.

"And then where?" you ask.

"Anywhere he tells us to go."

You follow Eleazar. Your legs feel wobbly, and your mouth has gone dry. You do not want other followers of Jesus to think that you have betrayed them, but you have to take this risk. You wonder if you will be brave enough to do whatever is required.

"There's Saul," Eleazar says. "They've already headed out." You follow behind them. At first, you do not realize what street you are on, until they stop outside of your house.

"No!" you scream. "Joshua! Anna! Get out! Run!" You continue screaming for your family to escape until you feel something heavy hit your head. You fall to the ground. A warm, sticky liquid drips into your eyes. You think it must be your own blood.

You lie in the street as the guards force their way into your house. You turn over to see if your family got away, but your head is spinning. You taste the dirt of the road, and you cannot lift your head.

Then you hear, "That foolish kid warned them. They've escaped!" You smile to yourself and let the blackness overtake you.

THE END

You race to Simeon's house, running over rooftops to save time. You jump down near his door and pound on it.

"Simeon," you gasp. "Simeon!"

Simeon opens the door. "What is it?"

"Soldiers are coming. They're coming to arrest you and your family because you're believers. You've got to leave now. They're almost here."

"Shomer! Maacah!" Simeon calls. Within seconds, his wife and daughter are beside you in the street. You look over your shoulder. You can hear footsteps in the distance. Simeon whispers, "Take them with you. I will remain to stall for time."

You do not argue. There is no time. You walk quickly down the street with Shomer and Maacah. You are only houses away when you hear pounding on Simeon's door. You force yourself not to look back and continue at the same pace. Whatever happens, you must not draw attention to yourselves.

"They are there," Maacah whispers. "They are at our house. Father is still inside. What is going to happen to him?" Her voice slowly begins to rise. "What is going to happen to us? How are we going to survive? Will we ever see father again?"

You say, "Shomer, go to the house on the center section of the old wall by Elias' house. Do you know where I mean?" You see her nod, and you continue, "Joshua and Anna are there. You can escape with them if we get separated."

Maacah's voice begins to rise. "What will

happen to Father?" You have to act fast. You push Maacah toward her mother.

CHOICE ONE: If you leave your friends and then attract the soldiers' attention somewhere else, go to page 34.

CHOICE TWO: If you put your hand over Maacah's mouth and continue at a slow pace, go to page 93.

From the road, you head north. As soon as you are out of sight of Jerusalem, you take off Anna's clothes and tie them into your tunic. You feel so much cooler.

You walk quickly. Your family could not be far ahead. They are pulling a heavy cart. You know, because you packed it well. By late afternoon, you catch up to them.

Naomi runs to you and holds you tightly. "I thought we would never see you again," she says. Joshua and Anna are next. Little Rachel is holding her arms up to you with her fingers wiggling back and forth.

"Carry me," she says.

You have been part of this family for such a short time, and yet they all love you. You thank God for them. Deep inside, you feel guilty about escaping through the window and leaving your family at the mercy of the guards. You place Rachel on the cart and pick up the handles to push.

"How about a ride?"

Rachel squeals in delight.

"I was going to hide the cart for you outside of Jerusalem. That's when I saw you leaving. I couldn't bring it to you because Saul's men were looking for me."

"How did you get out then?" Naomi asks.

You stop the cart. From within your tunic, you untie Anna's old clothes. You put them back on and hobble around the cart. Everyone laughs.

After several days, Joshua finds work as a carpenter in a small village in Judea. You also work hard to help your family, and whenever you get the chance, you tell people about Jesus.

THE END

"Mahol, Beker left to alert the authorities," you say.

Mahol nods. "Then I'd better talk faster." He continues preaching and two others choose to follow Jesus. When the footsteps of officials draw close, all but the four of you flee.

The soldiers drag you to prison and throw you into a cell together. Then they take you out one by one. When it is your turn, your hands are tied to a metal loop. A guard takes his leather whip and flails it at your back.

"Ouch!" you cry involuntarily. The metal on the ends of the leather cuts into your back. The strokes continue. At the 39th lash, you feel as if you are going to pass out.

Then suddenly, they stop hitting you. They throw you back into your prison cell. It is cooler there and smells musty. The others have been beaten, too.

The pain is worse than you have ever felt before, but you feel like laughing. Your friends join in. The joy of Jesus is everywhere. You teach the others a couple of songs. Every time you take a breath, the cuts on your back sting. Still, you want to praise God for saving Mahol and your two other friends. You all sing for about an hour.

The next morning, the soldiers release you with the warning, "Don't let us catch you telling others about Jesus!"

"I must obey God, no matter what you ask me to do," Mahol says. You prepare to be thrown back into prison, but they let you go anyway.

The four of you decide to leave Jerusalem. As you head out the gate together, Mahol says, "People all over the world need to hear about Jesus. Where should we start?"

You laugh. "Wherever the road leads, I guess."

With joy in your hearts, the four of you follow the road together.

THE END

You stay near Stephen and watch the other man drawing closer to you.

When he gets close enough to hear you, you say, "Good riddance."

The man raises his eyebrows. "What are you doing?"

You give a smile without humor. "I wanted to make sure this blasphemer was dead."

"I'm Eleazar," he says. You nod to him.

"I saw you with Saul earlier," you say. "I think that's his name. Is he in charge?" You walk out of the ditch toward Eleazar. You hope he cannot see how badly your legs are shaking.

"Saul is our leader," he said. "Thanks to him, things are going to change around here."

"How?" you ask. You both begin walking back toward Jerusalem. Part of you hates to leave Stephen's body alone, even though you know his spirit is with Jesus in Paradise.

"We're going to raid the homes of blasphemers, these followers of Jesus," he says. "It's a false religion. We need to wash our country clean of them—in blood, if necessary."

"I see," you say. He is eyeing you suspiciously. You can feel yourself beginning to sweat.

"You can join us if you like," he says.

CHOICE ONE: If you do not join Saul's men, go to page 85.

CHOICE TWO: If you join Saul's men, go to page 46.

"Help me!" you call to Beker and Mahol. The three of you quickly work together to climb up the side of a house. Within moments, you are running along the rooftops. Then without a word, you split up and run in different directions. You have done this routine so many times with your friends in the past. The sun's heat beats on your back. You jump down near the home of Simeon, a friend of Joshua's.

Keeping a careful eye, you work your way to Rabbi Levi's house and then dart into the alley behind it. A slight breeze goes by you. The fragrance of flowers is all around you. This is one of your old hangouts. It is not long before your other two friends meet you there.

Mahol says, "I hope what you stole was worth the trouble."

You hold out empty hands. "I didn't get anything for it."

"Oh," says Beker in disgust. "You mean we went through that and now have to hang low for nothing?"

Mahol says, "It's not like you to come back empty-handed. Why were those guards after you?"

CHOICE ONE: If you tell your friends that you are a follower of Jesus, go to page 66.

CHOICE TWO: If you shrug and change the subject, go to page 38.

"You'd better pack while I scout for an escape route," you tell your family.

Joshua agrees, "I do not know what we'd do without you." Joshua and Anna have meant so much to you. It makes you feel good that you are able to help them, too. You give Joshua a hug before you leave the house.

Once on the street, you weave in and out of buildings and behind and over houses to find the right section of wall where your family can climb down. In an older area of town, you find a house on the wall of Jerusalem that you can easily climb. Even Rachel should be able to climb it with Anna's help. The way up this building is at the end of a narrow lane. It is dark and will keep you hidden from probing eyes.

"Now all I need is rope," you say to yourself. You go to the market and ask around.

"I'll give you some used rope," a merchant says, "in exchange for help unloading my carts." You inspect the used rope. It will work.

"I'll do it," you say. You think it is a good trade until you realize how many carts of vegetables he has. Sweat drips from your face. Splinters from the carts pierce your hands. It takes you hours to complete the task, but once it is done and you have the rope, you thank the man.

After carrying and lifting vegetables, your muscles are sore. The ropes feel heavy. You wrap them diagonally around your left shoulder and waist and hurry back to the building where your family will make their escape.

The ropes throw you off balance as you climb. The palms of your hands throb with the pain of blisters. About halfway up, you miss your footing. You touch only air. You hang by your fingers. The ropes grow heavier and heavier. They are weighing you down. You scramble with your feet for a ledge until you find one. Whew! That was close.

You continue climbing. You are almost to the roof—just one more reach with your arm. One rope starts slipping from its loop as someone comes out of the building. He walks directly below you. You hold tightly to the wall and try not to move so that you do not draw attention to yourself. When he is gone, you manage to swing yourself over the top edge of the roof.

Once you have checked the roof to make sure that it is safe, you look for a place to go down the outside wall. A large stone jutting from the inside top of the wall is perfect for tying the rope. You attach it and then cover the coil with hay stored on the roof. When your family arrives later, all you will have to do is let the rope down over the wall to the ground outside the city. You hide a second rope under the hay. Everything is set. You go home. The family is packed.

"We'll have to split up to avoid suspicion," you say.

Joshua nods. "We can meet after dark. Where

should we meet?"

You explain to them where to go. Now all you have to do is wait. Anna and Naomi visit a friend. Joshua and Rachel stay at the house. You wait behind Rabbi Levi's house. Time passes slowly. Finally it begins growing dark. It is only moments now. You can feel your heart beating faster. Your hands are growing clammy. In the dimming light, you hear men talking behind a courtyard wall.

"When Benjamin gets here, we will go to Simeon the stonecutter's house. He's a follower of Jesus. We'll make an example of his family."

You know Simeon. He is a good man and a friend of Joshua. He is in great danger. If you warn Simeon, you could be putting your family in danger. If you do not warn Simeon, his family will be harmed. What should you do?

CHOICE ONE: If you warn Simeon, go to page 49.

CHOICE TWO: If you take care of your family, go to page 20.

You fling the door open and try to fight the soldiers. You know that you are no match for their strength or their numbers.

"Run!" you scream. One hits your face with a stick. You ignore the pain. If only your family can escape, then the pain will be worth it. Another pushes you roughly from the doorway. You yell again, "Run! Run!"

The other soldiers push past you. You fall. They step on your hands and arms as they rush to grab Joshua, Anna, Naomi, and Rachel. Rachel starts to cry. You know she is afraid. A soldier knocks dishes to the ground. Another smashes the chair that Joshua made for Anna.

You sit up and try to fight harder, holding onto the legs of those around you. Again you are knocked to the floor before they drag you to prison. Once you are all in the prison cell, Anna examines your sores and bruises.

"You shouldn't have fought them," she says gently. Your cuts have stopped bleeding, but your body pulsates with pain.

"I must have led them to the house when I ran home to tell you about Stephen," you say. "I wasn't thinking. I'm sorry."

Joshua puts a hand on your shoulder. You wince but are glad to feel his strength. "We are glad you came home to tell us."

"Mommy, I'm scared," Rachel says. Anna opens her arms, and Rachel climbs into them.

Anna says, "Let's sing together." Her voice starts softly. Joshua joins her. Soon you are singing, too. You know your days on earth may be numbered, but you feel God's peace as you sing. You would not want to be anywhere else than in his presence, which is where you are right now.

THE END

You sneak back into your family's house. In the rag box, you find an old dress and veil that belonged to Anna. It is full of holes, but you wrap yourself in it, trying to look like a field worker. You leave your own clothes on underneath.

Then you search the house until you find a ragged-looking basket. You place it under your arm and walk toward the city gate. Maybe if you hobble a little, you will be more convincing. In fact, if you are bent over, you can hide your face! You try it.

"Old woman," the gatekeeper says as you draw near to the gate. "Bring me some garlic when you return."

It worked! He must think you are going to work in the fields. You grunt as if in answer and then pass through the gate.

CHOICE ONE: If you head north to find your family, go to page 51.

CHOICE TWO: If you go into the fields and start working to avoid suspicion, go to page 83.

"That's great, Mahol," you say. "I wish I could go with you, but I have to find my family."

"I understand," Mahol says. "God has different work for each of us to do."

After spending a few more days together, you set off in opposite directions. You travel wherever the dusty road takes you, in search of your family. You survive on fish and the kindness of other believers in the areas where you travel. You look for ten years, all the time keeping Mahol and your family in your prayers. It is a solitary life, but you grow closer to God through it. Wherever you go, you tell people about Jesus. After ten years of searching, you find your family in a small village on the outskirts of Judea.

Anna recognizes you immediately, "You have come home!" Soon Joshua wraps his strong arms around you. You did not realize how much you had missed them. You cry tears of joy. Soon Rachel and Naomi are hugging you, too. They have grown much taller.

You settle down in their village and become a basket weaver and storyteller. The village children gather around every day to hear the stories of your travels and how God used you to bring people to Jesus Christ. Life is very, very good.

THE END

"Those guards were about to arrest my adopted father," you say.

"Joshua did something wrong?" Beker asks. You are surprised that she knows his name.

You shake your head no. "He is a follower of Jesus."

Mahol nods, knowingly. "Saul asked the Council for permission to hunt down Jesus' followers."

"We were going to leave Jerusalem, but they recognized Joshua. I had to think of something fast so he could get through the gate."

Beker takes a step away from you and acts like she's studying the rough stones in the wall. "So you're a follower, too?"

"Yes."

"I'm getting out of here," she says, and darts away.

Mahol hesitates, looking like he might leave, too. Then he turns around and sits on the ground beside you. "I'd like to ask you some questions. What makes this Jesus fellow so important? Why is the town so divided on who this one man is?"

"Because he isn't just a man. He's God," you say. Mahol wants to understand. You talk together late into the night. Finally he says, "I want to follow Jesus, too."

You smile. "Then tell Jesus you're sorry for your sins and that you believe he is God."

"In case you haven't noticed, Jesus isn't here,"

he says.

"You tell him from your heart," you say.

You both hear footsteps. "I will," he promises. His face looks concerned, and he immediately scrambles up the wall next to you.

Suddenly guards grab your hands. You are so surprised that you do not fight back.

They throw you into prison. The floor is hard and feels cold. You shiver most of the night and catch a cold. After a few days, your cold worsens. You begin to cough a lot. Then one day, you are allowed a visitor. Mahol walks in with a smile.

Even before he whispers, "I'm a follower of Jesus now," you can tell he is because of the joy in his eyes. He continues, "I'll find a way to get you out of here."

You shake your head no. "Find my family," you say. "Tell them that I'm okay."

"But I can't leave you here," he says. "I have a plan to help you escape."

"No," you say. "I want to stay here. If I escape, that soldier over there would be killed. He's responsible. I've been telling him about Jesus. He doesn't like hearing it, but maybe he'll listen after a while. I've been praying for him."

Mahol looks at you strangely. "I've never met anyone like you."

"It's only Jesus who makes me act like this," you say. "Please go to my family."

Mahol nods. "All right, but I'll see you again."

You nod. "If not on earth, then in heaven."

As he leaves, it almost looks like there is a tear sliding down his face. You give him a smile. You are glad that he is gone, because you can feel your cough coming back. You cough deeply and cannot seem to stop. It hurts to breathe. You know you are dying.

The soldier gives you a drink of water. It is the first kindness he has shown you. Each day, you get worse and worse, but you still pray for the soldier and tell him how much God loves him. You thank him for taking care of you.

Then one day, the soldier says, "Why do you care so much about me? I've done little for you."

"Because Jesus lives in me, and he loves you more than you can imagine."

The soldier listens while you explain how Jesus can save him from his sins and give him eternal life with God. Just before you die, you have the joy of knowing that the soldier has become a brother in Christ.

THE END

Although you want to scream, you hold it in. You try to blend into the crowd. It seems like forever until the angry men around you leave for the city. From what they say, you can tell they think they just did something pleasing to God. You know that the penalty for blasphemy is death by stoning, but Stephen would never dishonor God or his name.

You do not want to draw suspicion to yourself, so you start toward the city with the others. When no one is looking, you circle back around and hurry to Stephen's side. You hope he is alive.

You struggle to lift the heavy stones off his body. He does not seem to be breathing.

"Stephen, I'm here," you say. "Wake up."

He does not move. "Are you dead? Please don't be dead."

Just then you look up. In the distance, a man is watching you. He was one of the men with Saul. You try to find any sign of life in Stephen. His body is still warm, but he is dead. You stand up.

CHOICE ONE: If you trick Saul's follower into believing you are one of them, go to page 55.

CHOICE TWO: If you go back into Jerusalem, go to page 70.

You look away from the man and hurry back to Jerusalem by another route. Once inside the city, you know that you cannot return to your family's home. That would put them into too much danger.

With a sigh, you go back to living on the streets. You plan to leave Jerusalem, but you want to warn your family first. You hang out near the Temple and meet up with Mahol.

"Where have you been, stranger?" Mahol knows how to find information. You tell him about your new home with Joshua and Anna.

"I've seen you with them," he says.

You point to the Council chamber. "What's going on inside?"

"The Council just gave Saul the power to put people into prison."

"Who? What people?" you ask. You hope you sound casual enough not to make him suspicious. You lean against the smooth wall surrounding the chamber.

"The followers of Jesus. Weren't you one of them? Hey, maybe there's a reward out for you."

You laugh. "There's no reward. Who would want me?"

Mahol laughs. "Just asking."

"I would like to get a message to the family I was with," you say. "I want them to know that I'm safe. But living with them ... well ... they need to know I'm not coming home. And if what you say is true, they need to leave town."

"They were good to you, weren't they?" Mahol asks.

"They were great," you say.

"Why don't you want to go back?"

"It's a long story." You stare at the Temple steps.

CHOICE ONE: If you do not tell him the true reason, go to page 40.

CHOICE TWO: If you tell him the truth, go to page 27.

You go back to your family's house and pray. Saul's men may be watching the house, so you stay out of sight. You ignore your growling stomach and spend all your time praying to God for the release of your family.

Finally, you clean yourself up, straighten the house, and pack everything that is of value. You find an old cart in back and load all of your family's belongings onto the cart. You plan to hide the cart in the hills outside of Jerusalem. Everything will be waiting for them whenever they get out of prison.

You leave and walk boldly down the street with the cart. You are strong enough to easily hold the handles and keep everything in its place. You know that God is with you. You see others looking at you strangely and notice that you are drawing too much attention. You park the cart in an alleyway and hide. From the coolness of the shadows you watch.

You notice guards are escorting some people through the gates, forcing them to leave the city. You are overjoyed to see that Joshua, Anna, Rachel, and Naomi are among them. You breath deeply. God has been so good to you.

You see Beker behind you and wave to her. "Over here."

She joins you. "Long time no see."

You nod. "I need your help." When you explain, she rolls her eyes, but takes the cart out of the city to Joshua.

When Beker returns, she tells you, "I don't

think your family was expecting their things. They seemed pretty surprised." She backs up as if she is going to leave.

"Thank you," you say. You give her a wide smile. "You've done a very good thing today."

She shrugs. "They seemed happy to hear that you were safe." She stops as if a fight is going on inside of her. "Oh, here." She plops something into your hand. It is Anna's gold ring. "They wanted you to use this for money until you can get to them." She turns to leave, but you grab her hand and put the ring back into it.

"God gives me everything I need," you say. "Take this in payment for what you did for me and my family." You see a moment of uncertainty in Beker's face before she smiles and closes her fist over the ring.

"Your loss," she says and disappears into the crowd.

Your prayers have been answered. Your family has escaped. Unfortunately, Saul's men are still looking for you.

CHOICE ONE: If you sneak out of Jerusalem in a merchant's cart, go to page 23.

CHOICE TWO: If you dress like a field worker and try to go through the gate, go to page 64.

You take a deep breath. It would feel so good to try to get back at Saul and his followers for what they did to your family. Just then you remember Stephen's words. "Do not hold this sin against them." You try to concentrate on your family and not on your anger.

As soon as you arrive back at the house, you begin packing your few belongings.

Joshua smiles. "I'm glad you will be with us."

"Where will we go? What will we do?" you ask.

"Wherever God tells us to go and whatever God tells us to do."

You had forgotten that God was still in charge. You help Naomi tie her belongings into a blanket. Many things must be left behind. You take only what you can carry. With one last look at the only home you have ever known, you head for the nearest gate with your family. For a moment, it is a little tense. The gatekeepers are checking everyone. You see them eyeing Anna's face. Her veil does not quite hide the cuts and bruises.

"It isn't going to work," you say under your breath to Joshua.

Joshua puts his hand on your arm. "Sometimes when things seem their worst, God is doing his best." You are behind a cart of garlic. One step. Two steps. After the cart owner is a man on a horse, and then your family is next. You try not to look at the guards.

"Hey you," says one of the soldiers. He is pointing at Joshua.

Just then, the cart of garlic stops abruptly. The horse bumps into the cart. It tips. Garlic spills everywhere. In the confusion, you and your family walk through the gate without being stopped. You turn back to see what caused the commotion. The donkey pulling the cart had sat down and was refusing to move.

You want to laugh and yell and dance, but you follow Joshua at a slow pace. As much as you try to stop it, a grin breaks out on your face.

Joshua looks at you and his eyes twinkle. "It isn't the first time that God used a donkey to deliver his people."

The air is fresh. The sun is warm. It does not matter where you are headed. The Lord will guide you. You are overjoyed to be alive and with your very own family.

THE END

"I'll go with you," you say. You want to find your family, but there is little chance of meeting up with them again. Mahol has helped you see how important it is to tell others about Jesus. You would never have believed that Mahol would become a follower. Perhaps more of your friends would believe if you could find the courage to tell them. You pray for that courage.

You both join a caravan that is heading toward Jerusalem. One by one, each member of the caravan hears about God's Son, Jesus, from Mahol. Although no one chooses to believe, they seem to like Mahol. Once you have reached the outskirts of Jerusalem, the leader draws you and Mahol aside and gives you both a sweet, gritty fig to chew on while he talks.

"Do not be so loud in your praise of Jesus once you are in Jerusalem. I wish you to live long lives."

Mahol gives him a grin. "Thank you for your concern, but with Jesus, we have eternal life already. Remember, you can have it, too."

Once inside, you go in search of your old friends. Beker and five others are hanging out in an alley.

"Guess what!" Mahol says. "I have to tell you about something exciting. I have met God through his Son, Jesus Christ."

Because everyone respects Mahol, they listen. After a while, you see Beker slowly moving away from the group. In the pit of your stomach, you feel that she is going to tell the officials that Mahol is a follower of Jesus.

CHOICE ONE: If you tell Mahol what Beker is doing, go to page 53.

CHOICE TWO: If you follow Beker, go to page 89.

Although it is late afternoon by the time you all have your belongings packed, the gate is still open. As a family, you decide to leave immediately. After Stephen's stoning, the thieves in the surrounding hills seem less scary than the religious leaders inside Jerusalem.

You separate from one another so you will not draw attention to yourselves. First Anna and Rachel leave through the gate together. No one questions what they are doing. You breathe a sigh of relief. Then Naomi walks through. She has all her belongings in a basket on her head. Although it is the wrong time for girls to go out to the fields, you hope the guards will think she is a worker. She passes through the gates without drawing attention to herself.

Casually leaning against a stall in the market, you wait. Joshua begins his walk through the marketplace and toward the gate. Just then you see two men pointing to Joshua. They are talking together and nodding their heads.

CHOICE ONE: If you signal Joshua with a whistle to tell him there is trouble, go to page 87.

CHOICE TWO: If you create a diversion, go to page 30.

You want to protect your friends, so you go back down the alley to try and escape. A soldier is waiting for you at the end.

"No one steals while I'm on watch," he says.

He holds you in a vice-like grip. It is impossible to get away from him. He throw you into prison. It is dirty. It is dank. It is dark.

For some odd reason, though, you are not depressed. You feel God's peace inside of you. As you sit there in the dark, you praise God and pray for your family and all the believers in Jerusalem.

Then, just as you are getting sleepy, you see a bright light. You hear praises to God, even though the cell remains quiet. An angel appears at your cell door. A sweet fragrance like spring flowers surrounds you. The angel motions for you to follow him. You think you must be dreaming. You follow the angel out of prison and to the gates of Jerusalem. The angel opens the gates and then shuts them softly behind you. When the gates shut, the sounds, smells, and light disappear.

You rub your eyes. You have escaped! Nothing is impossible for God!

You do not know where you are headed or if you will find your family, but that does not worry you. God is in charge. Wherever you go and whatever you do, he will provide.

THE END

In the morning, you leave early so that no one will see that you were at Hannah's house. You do not want her to get into trouble, too. You find an alley across from the prison where you can watch the guards coming and going. Pressing your body against the rough walls, you hide in the shadows. You notice who has the prison keys and who does not.

That night, you stay in the alley. You sleep on the dusty ground and watch the soldiers whenever you are not sleeping. In the middle of the night, you see your opportunity. One of the prison guards is sitting so that his right side is facing the alley across from you. You weave around back streets and between buildings to get to that alley. As silently as you can, you creep close to him. The prison keys are attached to a leather rope tied to his belt.

Who would have thought that your training as a thief would come in so handy? You have never stolen anything from a guard before now. Slowly you ease up behind him. You are within inches. His back leans against the building, and his arms are crossed over his chest.

If you can just untie the leather band, then the keys will be yours. Slowly you work the leather so that the soldier cannot feel your tugs. Just as you are about to get the key ring, there is a noise to the soldier's left.

He stands up quickly. As he does so, the key ring falls to the ground. The sound seems enormous to your ears. You think about grabbing the keys and running, but know that you would be caught. You melt into the alley's shadows. The soldier picks up the ring and re-ties it. You retrace your steps back to your place on the other side of the street.

For two days you watch for another opportunity, but none appears. Finally one day you see your new family being released from prison. When they are a few blocks from the prison, you join them. As you draw closer, you can tell that Anna and Joshua have been beaten. They are glad to see you.

"We didn't know what happened to you. How did you get away?"

"Through the window. I've been trying for days to find a way to rescue you."

"They warned us never to talk about Jesus again," Anna says.

"Are you going to obey them?" you ask.

"No!" little Rachel says. Everyone laughs, but you can feel anger welling up inside of you. This is your family. They are good people. They should not have been treated so badly just because they believe in Jesus.

Joshua tells you that they must leave Jerusalem. "Will you be coming with us?"

CHOICE ONE: If you leave Jerusalem with your family, go to page **74.**

CHOICE TWO: If you stay in Jerusalem to try to sabotage the men who are persecuting followers of Jesus, go to page **36.**

You go into the fields and start working. You tear out what you think are weeds.

A woman shouts, "Why are you pulling up the barley? Do you want to starve us all? Get out of here!"

How could you know? You have never worked in the fields before. Until a few months ago, you were just a street kid. Anna's clothes start slipping off. A girl not far from you starts laughing and pointing. You throw off Anna's bulky clothes and run for the hills. Everyone is laughing. No one follows.

You hide out in the hills for a few days. You eat figs from a tree and drink water from a neighboring farmer's well. You do not know where your family went, but you believe that God will keep them safe. In the morning, you find a road and follow it. Whatever direction it takes you, you are determined to serve the Lord as long as you live.

THE END

When you are sure that both Beker and Mahol are asleep, you sneak out of the house through the back window. You dart in and out of shadows through the streets of Jerusalem until you find a place in the wall to climb down the other side.

Once free, you realize that you have nowhere to go. You have concentrated so hard on escaping that you never even considered what you would do once you left. You decide that Samaria is as safe a place as any. Perhaps you will discover news of your family there.

You find a cave in the hills where you can sleep that night. Tomorrow, you will take the first step into your new life.

THE END

You know that if you do not offer to help Saul, this man will suspect you are a follower of Jesus. Still, you look down and shake your head.

"No," you say. "I'm not ready for that."

He shrugs. "To each his own."

When he leaves, you turn around and go back outside the city. You cannot put your family at risk by going home. You walk for a while, not knowing what to do. The path is hard and dusty. As you walk, a plan forms in your head. You can live off the land and keep an eye on the road. If your family leaves the city, you will be able to spot them. You think you know which road they will use.

You find a place that is high enough for you to see the road, but low enough so that others will not find you. Waiting is difficult. You have always preferred action. Now all you can do is pray. On second thought, that is the best thing you can do. When you are not hunting for food, you spend your time praying for your family and the other believers in Jerusalem.

Weeks go by, and then one day, you see them. You wait for your family to get a safe distance from the gate before you run down the hill toward them.

"Joshua! Anna!" you shout.

They are surprised to see you.

When Anna and the girls finally stop hugging you, Anna says, "We thought you had been killed. Where have you been?"

You tell them about what happened after Stephen was stoned. "I was afraid they would hurt you because of me." They hug you again and again. As a family, you leave for another area far away from Jerusalem.

THE END

You whistle to signal to Joshua that he is in trouble, but it is too late. The two men move forward. Two guards are with them. Everything happens at the same time. The guards grab Joshua's arms. Joshua sees you running forward to help. Your eyes meet.

In a loud voice, he says, "Do as you like to me. God gave me a brave child to take care of my family when I am gone!"

You stop. Joshua said those words not to the guards but as a message for you. He wants you to leave and help Anna and your sisters escape. Your heart aches. You hear Joshua struggling with the soldiers. You want to save him, but what can you do? Although you feel a horrible pain in your heart, you obey Joshua. His arrest has created the confusion you need to walk through the gates without being stopped.

"They got Joshua," you tell Anna. "He told me to take care of you."

You can see the tears in her eyes, but she nods and takes the hands of each of her girls.

"We'll wait for him in Samaria," you say, but you have little hope of seeing him. Once again Anna nods, as if she cannot trust her voice.

In Samaria, you find work as a shepherd and take care of your family all of your days. You never see Joshua again. When you remember him, you thank God for giving you a father, even for such a short time. Joshua showed you God's love first-hand.

Throughout your life, you try to follow his example and show that same love to others.

THE END

You trail Beker so that she does not know you are following her. From the direction she is heading, you can tell that she is going directly to the Council. You wonder if she has been one of their spies all along. She would be able to tell them where the followers of Jesus lived. She is smart enough. Just before she goes into the building, you dive for her, and the two of you wrestle on the street.

When she stops struggling, you hold her down and ask her, "What are you doing?"

Her lips tighten. She does not say a word.

"You can turn me in, if you like," you say, "but leave Mahol and the others out of it." Beker turns her head away from you. You continue, "You know ... Jesus died for you, too."

"More lies," she says.

"The truth," you say. You have gotten dirt in your mouth, but there is nowhere for you to spit it out.

Beker struggles again, but you do not release your hold. "You don't care about your friends," she says. "You went and lived with Joshua and Anna. Then you took Mahol away. You both deserted me."

You never realized how alone Beker must have felt. "I'm sorry. I should have included you. Beker, Jesus really does love you. He died so that you can be forgiven for all your sins." You let go of her and sit on the ground beside her. She sits up.

"I don't believe it. He can't forgive me. I've done too many bad things."

You put your arm around her shoulders.

"We've all done too many bad things. That's why Jesus had to come. He would have come even if you were the only one who needed him. That's how much he loves you."

She looks away. You are not sure why until you hear her sniffle. She is trying to hide her tears. You have never seen this softer side of Beker.

You give her time to get control of her emotions before you say, "Beker, let's go back to Mahol."

She nods. You walk back together in silence. Seven days later when you leave Jerusalem, five of you leave as followers of Jesus. Beker is one of the five.

You travel together to Samaria, and you find your family already living there.

"You are good children," Anna says. "Joshua, can't we do something for each of them?"

"I don't know," Joshua says. "But I was talking with Gideon the other day. He's a brickmaker. He was looking for a young man who would want to learn his trade."

Mahol's eyes light up. Joshua smiles. "Mahol, would you be interested?"

"Oh, yes," he says.

"And I know someone who has always wished for a daughter," Anna says. "Would you be interested, Beker?"

"A family? A family of my own? Oh, please, yes!" She hesitates. "Would you please introduce me as Rebecca?" Everyone laughs.

"Of course."

By the end of the year, each one of the former street kids has found a trade or a family in the community.

THE END

You tell your boss you will be leaving with Palti, who has now become your friend. He sends someone else to watch the sheep. Originally, you thought that Palti was fleeing Jerusalem because he was scared, but after traveling with him for a few days, you realize that he is not afraid.

Warming his hands by the fire one night he says, "God has called me to go beyond Judea and preach the name of Jesus there."

"Do you mean that you left Jerusalem so that you can go tell others about Jesus?"

He nods.

"But what if they beat you or even kill you for what you say?" you ask. You do not tell him that you fled Jerusalem as a coward. What would he say if he knew that you were afraid of the Jewish leaders? You draw circles in the dirt.

Palti shrugs. "I've already been beaten and imprisoned. The worst they can do is kill my body. They can't take away my faith or God's Holy Spirit that lives inside me."

What he says makes sense. Although you do not want to go through the pain of persecution, you know that your life is in God's hands. Even if you die, he will take you to heaven to live with him forever.

"I'd like to learn to tell others about Jesus," you say.

Palti smiles. "You have plenty of time to learn. We're in for an amazing adventure."

THE END

You cover Maacah's mouth as you continue walking. Her spit gets on your hand, but you do not move your fingers.

Shomer grabs her daughter's arm. "Maacah, stop it. What if your father escapes only to find that we have been killed because you started to scream?"

Maacah's eyes suddenly clear. She relaxes. You pull your hand away and wipe it on your robe. You have not broken your stride.

Her mother continues. "God is with us even in our trouble. Trust him."

Shomer's words seem to calm Maacah even more. They help you, too.

You turn down one street and then another, looking behind you at every turn. When you are certain that you have not been followed, you go to the housetop where you hope your family is waiting. You are extremely late. You help Maacah and Shomer climb to the roof.

Joshua is waiting for you. Joshua has already let down Anna and the girls. You greet each other warmly but silently. You can see a question in his eyes when he sees Shomer and Maacah. He looks for Simeon, but you shake your head.

He ties another rope securely, and you work together to help Shomer and Maacah down. Then you and Joshua climb down together. You hide the ropes the best you can. Perhaps others will need them after you.

Once you are away from the walls, you

explain, "Saul's men were after Simeon's family. I had to do something."

"I'm proud of you," says Joshua. "Thank you for helping our friends." It makes you feel warm inside that he trusts you and your decisions. He continues. "We will take Shomer and Maacah to Bethlehem. Then we will see where God leads us."

You nod. You do not care where you go, as long as you are with those you love.

THE END

Escape!

Spiritual Building Block: **Courage**

You can do the following things to become a champion for the Gospel:

Think About It:

Have you ever told a friend to watch a movie that you hated? Have you ever talked for hours about a book you couldn't stand? Of course not! If you want to endorse something, you have to believe in it. The same thing goes with sharing your faith. Spend time in prayer and Scripture everyday, praying that the Holy Spirit will reveal himself to you, so that you will become a person of great faith.

Talk About It:

When you are excited about something, you naturally want to tell people about it. As you grow more in love with God, you will see all kinds of exciting things happen. When you tell your friends about what God has done for you, you don't have to try to convince them to become a Christian; you just have to tell them what you know. The Holy Spirit will do the rest.

Try It:

Some people think integrity is good behavior. It is actually living out what you believe. So, if you are a person of integrity and you say that you love Jesus, you will try to walk in step with the Spirit. If you want your friends to know that your faith is for real, you have to do what you know is right, avoid what you know is wrong, and say you're sorry when you mess up. Not only will your friends trust you more, you will be a happier person.

COLLECT THEM ALL!

DEADLY EXPEDITION!

Imagine that your decisions determine whether you will ever enter the Promised Land.

You and your entire nation of Hebrew slaves have just escaped from the Egyptians and are heading toward the land that God has promised to give you. But when you reach the Red Sea, you look behind to see the entire Egyptian army closing in on you! You must make a choice. Will you stand and fight the Egyptian army? Or will you trust God and miraculously cross the sea on a dry path—only to face the possibility of battling yet another nation? You must make a choice.

ATTACK!

Imagine that your decisions have the power to determine the fate of your country.

One day, while you are guarding your family's sheep, a bully attacks you from behind and steals your prized possession. You must make a choice. You abandon the sheep and chase the bully and almost catch him when you both see a huge foreign army in the distance. You must make a choice. Do you forget the differences you have with the bully, or work together to see what the foreigners are up to? You must make a choice.

TRAPPED!

Imagine that your decisions have the power to determine whether your family will be saved from its enemies.

Your Aunt Rahab is one of your favorite people, but your father doesn't want you to spend time with her. You must make a choice. When you visit her house you discover that the enemy of your people have been using her house as a hide-out! You must make a choice. Do you listen to Rahab's reasons for helping the spies? Do you believe her when she says that you must stay with her to be safe? Not everyone in your family believes her. You must make a choice.